# TROUBLE at TABLE 5

## #6:
## Countdown to Disaster

Check out all the

# TROUBLE at TABLE 5

books!

#1          #2          #3

#4          #5          #6

Read more books by **Tom Watson**

#1-12          #1-5

HARPER **Chapters**

# TROUBLE at TABLE 5

## #6:
Countdown to Disaster

by **Tom Watson**

illustrated by
**Marta Kissi**

**HARPER**
*An Imprint of* HarperCollins*Publishers*

Dedicated to MEJ
(23DLISCAYG)

Trouble at Table 5 #6: Countdown to Disaster
Text copyright © 2021 by Tom Watson
Illustrations copyright © 2021 by HarperCollins Publishers
Illustrations by Marta Kissi

Library of Congress Control Number: 2021933203
ISBN 978-0-06-300453-5 — ISBN 978-0-06-300452-8 (pbk.)

Typography by Torberg Davern
21 22 23 24 25   PC/LSCC   10 9 8 7 6 5 4 3 2 1
❖
First Edition
33614082380568

# Table of Contents

# CHAPTER ONE

## IT'S COUNTING DAY

## IT WAS THURSDAY.

That's my counting day.

I almost picked Wednesday to be counting day because it has nine letters— the most of any day.

But nine is an odd number. And I like even numbers way more than odd numbers. That's because with odd numbers, there's always something left over. And who wants that?

Saturday is tied with Thursday for the next most letters—eight. That's an even number. I had to choose between those two days.

I didn't want counting day to be on the weekend. So Thursday is counting day.

After I woke up, I brushed my teeth with twenty-six sideway strokes and eighteen up-and-down strokes.

For breakfast, I had Froot Loops—that's my favorite cereal. I took the green and purple ones out of my bowl. They remind me of grapes.

I counted the orange, yellow, red, and blue Froot Loops left in my bowl. There were 129. I put one back in the box before eating.

When I met my best friends, Rosie and Simon, at the end of my driveway, they knew it was counting day. They totally get me. They didn't think it was strange when I walked to school with my head down as I counted the sidewalk squares.

Of course, I know how many sidewalk squares there are on the way to school.

There are 412. I've counted them, like, a million times. But it never hurts to be absolutely certain.

I can still talk with Rosie and Simon while I count. It's like one part of my brain does the counting while a different part of my brain listens and talks. The counting part is in the back part of my head, on the right side near the top. The listening and talking parts are along both sides.

I was on sidewalk square number sixty-eight when Rosie asked, "Did you guys remember your book reports?"

"I did," Simon said and patted his backpack. "I found a book about monster trucks at the library."

"Uh-oh," I said and stopped on sidewalk square number seventy-two.

I knew where my book report was—and it wasn't in my backpack.

It was on the kitchen counter. I set it there when I put my cereal bowl and spoon in the dishwasher. I had to count all the bowls and spoons inside—because, you know, it was counting day. Then I saw Simon and Rosie out the kitchen window. They were waiting for me at the end of my driveway. I ran out to meet them—and left my book report on the counter.

I crouched down to unzip my backpack.

"Did you forget it?" Simon asked.

"I *think* I did," I said. I searched for a few seconds. "I *definitely* did."

"We'll go back with you," Rosie offered.

"No, that's okay," I said. "But will you stay on this square? It's number seventy-two and I can just start counting again from here when I get back."

Rosie and Simon said they would.

I ran back home—and that's when the trouble started.

# CHAPTER TWO
## WE HAVE TO MOVE

**I HUSTLED HOME** and went into the kitchen. My book report was right where I left it on the counter. It was all about the story of Henry Sugar, by Roald Dahl. That is one of my all-time favorite stories. I like how the main character gets his brain to be super focused on things.

I put the report in my backpack, zipped it up, and headed to the foot of the stairs. I could hear Mom and Dad talking up there.

Well, they weren't quite talking. It was more like yelling. That's because Mom was blow-drying her hair. So they had to yell to hear each other.

"I had to come home to get my book report!" I called up the stairs. "I forgot it!"

They didn't respond. The blow-dryer and their own yelling was too loud for them to hear me. So I decided just to hurry back to Rosie and Simon.

But when I got to the front door I didn't go outside. That's because I heard Dad yell my name in a sentence.

"We're going to need to move all Molly's things," he yelled.

I took my hand off the doorknob.

"What?" I said and walked back to the staircase. "Move all my things?"

"We'll have to move our stuff too," Mom yelled back. The blow-dryer was still going full-blast.

I cupped my hand around my ear.

"It's got to be done," Dad yelled. "It will be here sooner than we know it."

I scrunched up my face and asked myself, "What are they talking about?"

"I'll have to leave my job," Mom said loudly.

"We'll get by," Dad said back just as loudly. "But it's all going to change. We'll all be in a different place, that's for sure."

10

"Leave her job?" I whispered and backed away from the stairs toward the front door. I opened it slowly and quietly, even though I knew there was no way they could hear me. "Different place?"

I heard one last bit of their conversation.

"How do you think Molly's going to react when we tell her?" Mom called over the blow-dryer.

"I don't know," Dad called back. Then a few seconds later, he said, "We have to move."

Oh. No. I didn't want to move. No way. No possible way.

I squeezed the door shut—and ran back to Rosie and Simon. They waved at me from sidewalk square seventy-two. I'd have to move away from my two best friends in the whole world.

They must have seen the look on my face as I got closer. When I got to them, Rosie asked, "What's the matter, Molly?"

"Yeah," Simon said. "What's wrong?"

"Everything," I answered. "I can't talk about it right now. I'll tell you at Table 5."

I was glad it was counting day. It gave me something to concentrate on.

. . . 73, 74, 75 . . .

I stepped off square seventy-two.

I said in my brain, "*Seventy-three, seventy-four, seventy-five . . .*"

It helped—but not a lot.

OH NO! NO WAY! WHAT WILL MOLLY DO NOW?

# CHAPTER THREE

## KEEP IT DOWN, TABLE 5

AFTER MR. WILLOW took attendance, he explained that healthy eating would be our science subject that day. He drew a plate with four sections on the whiteboard. He gave us twenty minutes to fill in the sections with different categories of food.

"I want you to think about what you eat during a typical week," Mr. Willow said, "and fill in the plate with those foods.

Then we'll look at a healthy eating plate and you can see how your diet compares to it."

It was kind of a fun assignment. We got to use our colored pencils and could draw all the food too. It was also a good project because we were allowed to talk quietly at our tables as we worked.

As we started to draw our plates, Rosie asked, "So what's happening, Molly? Something was really bothering you on

HEALTHY EATING PLATE

the way to school."

"Yeah," Simon said. "We could tell."

I didn't want to look at my two best friends as I told them my bad news.

"Something happened when I ran back to get my book report," I said and hunkered down even closer to my paper. I had sectioned off one part of my food plate for protein. I wanted to draw a fish and a chicken.

Simon asked, "What happened?"

BOOK REPORTS THIS AFTERNOON!

"Well, it's not like something *happened* happened," I said. I outlined my fish with a black colored pencil. "It was more like I *heard* something."

"What did you hear?" Rosie asked and grabbed an orange pencil to draw carrots.

"Mom and Dad were upstairs. They were talking really loudly because Mom was blow-drying her hair," I said. I colored my tasty fish blue and gave it some bubbles. "And I heard what they said."

"And?" Simon asked.

I got ready to look up at Simon and Rosie for the first time since we started our food plates. I made sure my eyes weren't too watery.

"They said," I answered and took a deep breath of air before looking up, "that we're going to move."

19

"What?!" Rosie yell-whispered.

"You can't!" Simon yelled. There was no *whisper* attached to his yell.

"Keep it down, Table 5," Mr. Willow called from the front of the classroom.

"Are you sure?" Rosie asked. I could tell that she really hoped I was wrong.

"Totally," I said and nodded. "They talked about moving all my stuff. And all their stuff too."

Simon said, "Maybe it's a mistake."

"It's not," I told him—even though I wished that was true. "Here's a direct quote from my dad: 'We have to move.'"

"This is bad," Rosie said.

I knew she was right.

"We have to do something to stop it," Simon said.

I knew he was right too.

I just had no idea what we could do.

# CHAPTER FOUR
## THE BASEMENT PLAN

ROSIE, SIMON, AND I kept our heads down while we worked on our food plates.

"Why do they want to move?" Rosie asked as she colored some green broccoli bunches.

"I think maybe Dad got a new job," I answered. I started to draw my chicken. "I heard Mom say she would quit her job."

"So what are we going to do?" asked

Simon. I couldn't see what he was drawing. But he squeezed a yellow colored pencil in his hand and scribbled really hard. The tip of his tongue stuck out from the corner of his mouth.

"I don't know," I answered honestly. My chicken didn't look very good. It looked like a dog with a beak. I erased it and drew an egg instead. Then I started on my fruit section—bananas and oranges.

Rosie didn't have any ideas. And neither did I.

But Simon did.

"We'll just trap them," Simon said without looking up.

Rosie and I stopped drawing and turned to look at him. He must have felt our gaze because he explained some more as he worked.

"We'll take their favorite foods and set little bits of it on each step headed down to your basement," Simon explained. "What are your mom's and dad's favorite foods?"

"Mom likes chocolate," I answered. "And Dad likes french fries."

"Great," Simon said, still scribbling away. "We'll get some french fries and chocolates and put them on your basement steps. We'll hide and watch your parents follow their favorite foods all the way downstairs."

25

"When they get to the basement, we sneak in and slam the door shut." Simon paused. "Then we'll lock it three or four times."

"You want me to capture my own parents?" I asked.

"It's not *bad* capturing," Simon said, finally looking up at Rosie and me. "It's *good* capturing."

"Umm, how is it good?" Rosie asked. She couldn't believe what Simon had suggested. Neither could I.

"We'll give them food and stuff," Simon explained. "Not like bread and water. Good food. Like spaghetti and meatballs and grilled cheese and Fruit Roll-Ups. And we'll toss down comic books and other fun stuff. Like a jump rope. Or some monster truck toys!"

"Simon, how long, umm, are we going to keep Molly's parents trapped in their own basement?" Rosie asked.

"Just until high school graduation," Simon answered. "By then, Molly will be going to Harvard or Stanford or wherever and her parents can move anywhere they want! Bingo-bango-bongo! Problem solved!"

I didn't know what to say. Neither did Rosie.

But, unfortunately, Mr. Willow did.

He was standing right behind Simon.

And that meant trouble at Table 5.

## CHAPTER FIVE

## SIMON IS . . . SIMON

WE HADN'T SEEN Mr. Willow coming.

"What problem did you solve?" he asked, crossing his arms against his chest as he stared down at Simon.

"Umm," Simon said, pausing for time. He leaned his head straight back and looked up at Mr. Willow.

"What problem did you solve?" our teacher repeated.

"Mr. Willow, can I ask you something?" Simon said, still leaning back. Rosie and I could tell he was going to try to change the subject. He knew that Mr. Willow wouldn't appreciate us talking about anything other than our food plates.

Mr. Willow didn't look like he wanted to hear what Simon was about to ask. But he said, "Okay, Simon. What is it?"

Then Simon said something I wouldn't have guessed in a million-billion years.

He asked, "Did you know that you have magnificent nostrils?"

"What?" Mr. Willow asked. He didn't ask *What?* because he hadn't heard Simon. He asked *What?* because he couldn't believe what had just come out of Simon's mouth.

"Your nostrils," Simon said. "They're *magnificent.*"

Mr. Willow put his right hand on his forehead and shook his head. He wasn't mad. He was more, like, amused. Mr. Willow was often amused by Simon. "You really think so, Simon?"

"For real," Simon said and sat back upright. "Your nostrils are nice and circular. Pretty symmetrical. Not too hairy. Excellent specimens, I'd say."

I stared down at my food plate as hard as I could. My eyes watered. Not from crying

over the move, but from trying really hard not to laugh out loud. Rosie felt the same way. She squeezed her eyes shut.

"Simon, sometimes I wonder if your brain and your mouth are connected," Mr. Willow said and smiled.

"I know, right?" Simon said and scrunched up his shoulders. He had successfully changed the subject.

Mr. Willow came around to the front of Table 5 and said, "Let's see how you three are doing with your food plates."

He looked at Rosie's first. And it was, as usual, awesome.

Mr. Willow looked at mine next.

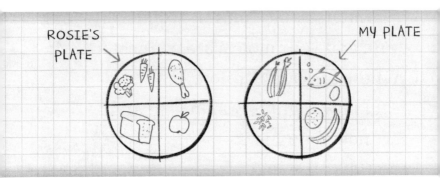

ROSIE'S PLATE

MY PLATE

"This looks good, Molly," he said, handing my food plate back after examining it for a few seconds. "But your fruit section is a little empty. Let's add one more. How about some grapes?"

"I don't eat grapes."

"You don't?" Mr. Willow asked. "Are you allergic?"

"No," I answered and explained some

more. "Grapes come in bunches. And I can't count how many are in a bunch. And I like to eat things in even numbers. So, obviously, I don't eat grapes."

"Right, umm, okay. That makes perfectly good sense," Mr. Willow said. "How about an apple then?"

"No," I answered again—and explained again. "I only eat fruit that is the same color on the inside and outside. An apple is red or green on the outside, but white on the inside. So no apples for me."

Mr. Willow asked, "How about two cherries?"

"Okay!" I said and reached for the red colored pencil.

Then Mr. Willow picked up Simon's food plate.

"Simon!" he exclaimed. "What is this?!"

# CHAPTER SIX
# THE MARSHMALLOW GROUP

MR. WILLOW STARED at Simon's paper.

"It's my plate," Simon answered simply. "With all my foods."

"I know what it is, Simon. I'm just trying to make sense of it," Mr. Willow said and pointed at the paper. "For instance, what are the white things in this section?"

"That's the marshmallow group," Simon answered. "There are big ones and little ones."

"And marshmallows are a big part of your diet?"

"Not a huge part," Simon said. "I only eat them maybe once or twice a day."

"Okay, umm," Mr. Willow said and pointed at a different section of Simon's food plate. "And what about these? Is this the fruit section?"

"Sort of."

"What do you mean, *sort of*?"

"They're not quite fruit," Simon said. "But they're fruit-*ish*."

"Aren't these cherries and grapes and lemons?"

"No."

"What are they?"

"They're Skittles," Simon said. "That's the Skittles group."

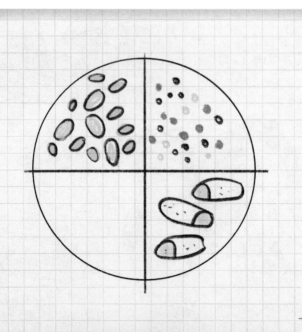

I think Mr. Willow decided he was done talking with Simon. He turned away from our table and headed back to the front of class. On his way, Mr. Willow called, "Okay, everybody. Time's up!"

Simon turned to Rosie and me. He had a disappointed look on his face. He pointed at another section of his plate and said, "Mr. Willow didn't even ask me about this group."

"What is it?" Rosie asked.

"It's the Twinkies group."

Rosie slapped her right hand across her mouth to keep from laughing. Simon's crazy food plate had made me forget all about having to move—but not for long.

"Time to get started," Mr. Willow said loudly. He was at the whiteboard with a bunch of colored markers. "Let's compare your personal eating habits with a plate that reflects a healthy diet. So we're looking at what you eat at home with your family versus a well-balanced diet."

*At home with your family.*

Mr. Willow's words got stuck in my head.

*At home with your family.*

"I don't want to move," I whispered to Rosie and Simon.

"Lunchtime," Rosie whispered. "We'll figure it out at lunchtime."

After science, we handed in our book reports for English and then had music. After that, it was lunch.

We found a table to ourselves. It was a good lunch day for me—lots of even numbers. There were two slices of cheese pizza, a banana that I broke into eight pieces, and five celery sticks. I gave one of those to Simon.

When I was done organizing everything on my tray, Simon said, "I know exactly what we can do."

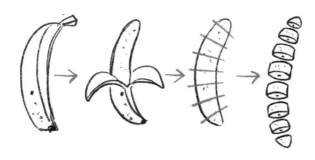

## CHAPTER SEVEN
# MONSTER TRUCK MEGA-PALOOZA

SIMON TOLD US his idea.

"It involves my favorite thing in the world," Simon began. "I call it Monster Truck Mega-Palooza!"

Rosie looked at me. I looked at Rosie. We were both worried about where this could go.

"I get a monster truck!" Simon began. He put his pizza slice down. "I drive it over to your house on moving day. I'll run over some mailboxes and garbage cans on the way! You know, smash stuff up and make a lot of noise. Then when the moving truck pulls into your driveway, I'll run over it and squash it to pieces!"

Rosie and I stared at him.

"If you don't have a moving truck to take your stuff away," he explained, "then you can't leave!"

"Umm, Simon," I said and tried to hide the disappointment on my face. I looked at Rosie. "You don't have a license. And you, umm, don't know how to drive."

"What's so hard about driving?" Simon asked. "Turn the steering wheel. Press the gas pedal. Run over stuff!"

I turned to Rosie for help—she was twirling her hair.

"Wait," I said. "Do you have an idea?"

"Something Simon said made me think of it," Rosie answered. "He said his plan would involve his favorite thing in the world. And I think if we remind your parents about all *their* favorite things around your house, then maybe they won't want to leave."

"What kinds of things?" I asked.

"Anything," Rosie answered. "Favorite rooms, favorite foods, things they like to do. You could even get them something from their favorite stores in town. Whatever."

"Could it be memories too?" I asked Rosie. I was starting to like this idea.

"Like the driveway where they taught me how to ride my bike? Stuff like that?"

"Yes!" Rosie exclaimed. I think she appreciated how I took her idea and expanded on it. "Memories are a great idea!"

"Let's remember that this all started with my monster truck idea," Simon said proudly. He stuck one end of his last celery stick in his mouth and asked, "But how is Molly going to make that work?"

"What do you mean?" I asked.

"Well, you can't just give them their favorite candy. Or sit them down on their favorite chair or whatever," Simon said. "There has to be a reason for them to find stuff. Or to remember when something special happened."

"You're right," Rosie said and started to twirl her hair again. "There needs to be a *way* for them to remember everything. A *reason*."

"Can I have some more of your celery?" Simon asked and pointed at my lunch tray. "I'm still hungry. I could take two pieces.

That way you'll still have an even number for yourself. I know it's counting day and everything."

I handed him two celery sticks.

"You can eat so much!" Rosie said and laughed. She wasn't teasing Simon. She just couldn't believe, you know, how much he could eat.

"I love celery," Simon said. He shrugged and took the celery from me. "Have you

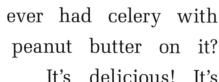

ever had celery with peanut butter on it? It's delicious! It's totally one of my favorite things!"

"That's it!" Rosie whispered and then snapped her head toward me. "Favorite things! Guess what you're going to do with your parents this weekend?"

"What?" I asked.

"All their favorite things!"

YOU'RE MORE THAN HALFWAY THROUGH! GREAT FOCUS!

## CHAPTER EIGHT

# TWO DONUTS, TWO BITES EACH

**THE PLAN WAS** to set up a whole day filled with my parents' favorite things—and special memories. We wanted to make it like a game. There would be clues and everything. It was a way to remind them of all the things they'd leave behind if we moved.

We had no idea if it would make them want to stay. But I definitely wanted to give it a try.

The first thing I had to do was make two lists. I did it during free time that afternoon.

I showed the lists to Rosie and Simon as we walked home.

"We have to make clues for each thing," Rosie said. "Like riddles or something. And we have to figure out what order they should be in."

That's what we did on Friday. We made clues—and we made a plan.

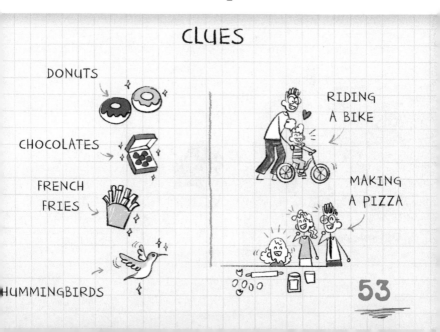

CLUES

DONUTS

CHOCOLATES

FRENCH
FRIES

HUMMINGBIRDS

RIDING
A BIKE

MAKING
A PIZZA

53

And on Saturday morning, we put the plan into action.

I woke up before Mom and Dad on purpose. I had to get a lot of stuff ready. I put all four clues in the right places. I turned the couch to face the hummingbird feeder. I moved the bikes out of the garage. Lots of stuff.

And I had to meet Rosie and Simon outside. They got up early too.

They came up the driveway while I

parked the bikes. Simon had two big cups of coffee. And Rosie had a box of donuts. Simon's mom waved to me from the sidewalk. She had a box of donuts too.

"Thanks for getting up early and going to the bakery," I said. "And helping me with this."

"We don't want you to move," Rosie said. "We'll do anything."

"Plus Hooshman's Bakery is my mom's favorite too," Simon said and wiped some chocolate from the corner of his mouth.

"Simon's already had two chocolate-covered donuts!" Rosie said and laughed. "He eats them in two bites!"

Simon smiled and shrugged. Then something caught his eye. He pointed toward my house. He said, "I think I just saw your dad walk past the window.

Your parents might be up."

"I have to go!" I said. I tucked the donut box under my arm and held a cup of coffee in each hand. "Thanks, you guys!"

"Good luck," Rosie said. "I hope it works."

"We'll be back with the french fries and chocolate later on," Simon said.

I nodded and hustled inside.

Mom and Dad were waiting for me.

Dad had the first clue in his hand.

# CHAPTER NINE

# THE GAME BEGINS

**I SET THE** coffee and donuts down inside the front door.

"Molly," Mom called from the living room. "What are you doing up so early? On a Saturday?"

"And what's this?" Dad said, holding up the envelope with the first clue inside. I had put it outside their bedroom door.

"It's your first clue!" I announced as I got to the living room. "We're going to play a game today. There are four clues that lead to four prizes.

"Sounds fun," Mom said and then eyeballed the living room. "Why is the couch turned around like this?"

"You have to open the first clue!"

They opened the first clue.

"Well," Mom said after they were done reading the clue. "Caffeine usually means coffee. Are you going to make coffee for us this morning?"

"Sort of."

"And maybe this bagel part means donuts?" Dad guessed. "Do you want me to go pick up donuts for breakfast?"

"Kind of."

"Okay, coffee and donuts, maybe," Mom said slowly, trying to put it all together. "But what does *Hummmmmm* mean?"

It's a game—with prizes!
Clue #1

A. Caffeine.
B. Shaped like a bagel (but better).
C. Hummmmmm.

I nodded at the couch and then out the window.

"Hummingbirds?" Dad asked.

"You guys sit on the couch," I said. "I'll be right back!"

I put the donuts on the table in front of

the couch. I gave them their coffees.

"Hooshman's Bakery?" Dad said, looking at the box. "Their donuts are the best!"

"Molly, you didn't go there by yourself, did you?" Mom asked.

"No," I answered and sat down between them on the couch. "Simon and Rosie went for me. Simon's mom took them."

We ate donuts for breakfast. I didn't have coffee. I had milk. Milk is really good with donuts. Mom and Dad ate donuts that had sprinkles on them. I didn't. There were way too many sprinkles to count and see if there was an even number. I had one chocolate-covered and one glazed.

"This is quite a treat," Mom said while we ate. "And look at the hummingbirds this morning. We should keep the couch turned this way all the time."

The day was off to a great start.

"Those aren't just *any* hummingbirds," I said. "Those are special Evanston, Illinois, hummingbirds."

"They *are* pretty," Mom said.

Then I asked, "Isn't Hooshman's the best bakery in the world?"

"It certainly is," Dad said.

"Time for the next clue!" I pulled the second envelope out from under the couch.

Clue #2

A. It may be blue,
   but it's not sad.
B. It happened on June 11.
C. Rhymes with "five day."

**"I HAVE NO** idea about the blue thing," Dad said. "But June eleventh is the day before your birthday."

Mom asked, "But what rhymes with five day?"

Dad made lots of guesses—lots of bad guesses.

"Strive clay?"

"Dive spray?"

"Thrive pay?"

"Jive gray?"

I had a feeling this would take a while, so I nodded toward the front window.

Our bikes were in the driveway. So was my very first bike. It looked really small next to my bike now. It was blue. When I first learned to ride it, I named it Blue Betsy for some reason. When I was little I liked to name stuff.

"Is that your first bike in the driveway?" Mom asked. "Blue Betsy?"

I nodded.

"Driveway!" Dad exclaimed and pointed at his head in a goofy way. "I'm a genius! I got it on the first try."

"Yeah, Dad. First try. Sure," I said, but he knew I was just kidding. "Do you guys remember when you taught me how to ride Blue Betsy when I was five years old? Because I didn't want to be six and still not know how to ride?"

"We remember," Mom said and messed up my hair a little bit.

"We were out in the driveway all day,"

Dad said and laughed. "You would *not* give up."

"I thought we could go on a bike ride together today," I said. "That's the second prize!"

And that's what we did. We rode almost every trail through Picasso Park—even the one that goes way down by the creek. When we got back, it was almost lunchtime.

"The trails at Picasso Park are the best," I said. "The absolute best!"

67

Mom and Dad agreed.

"I'm starving," Dad said after we put our bikes back into the garage.

"That's perfect," I said and pulled the next clue out of my pocket. I handed it to Mom. "You're going to like the next prize."

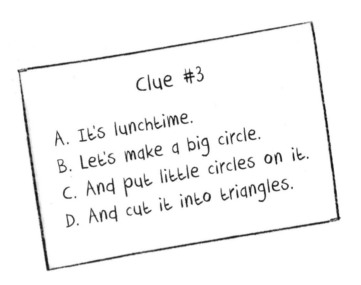

Clue #3

A. It's lunchtime.
B. Let's make a big circle.
C. And put little circles on it.
D. And cut it into triangles.

# CHAPTER ELEVEN

## PIZZA AND THE FINAL CLUE

MOM AND DAD figured out the next clue before we even got inside.

"We're going to make homemade pizza for lunch?" Dad asked. "That's the third prize, right?"

"Right. I got all the ingredients ready in the kitchen," I said. I needed to remind them of one memorable pizza-making experience in the past.

"Do you guys remember how bad the Great Pizza Dough Catastrophe was?"

"Do we?!" Mom exclaimed.

Dad laughed and asked, "Why do you think we named it the Great Pizza Dough Catastrophe?"

When I was little, we all made pizzas together. We made the dough with flour, yeast, warm water, salt, and olive oil. It's really easy to make. We made balls with the dough and then used rolling pins to spread our balls out into circles.

Mom and Dad both left the kitchen at

the same time for a couple of minutes. While they were gone I decided to throw and spin my pizza dough above my head like a professional pizza chef.

I didn't catch it right or it was too flimsy or something.

And the pizza dough fell over my head.

"Mom! Dad!" I yelled through the dough covering my face. "I need some help."

Mom and Dad weren't mad. They thought it was hilarious. They took tons of pictures. When the dough was over my face, Dad said I should eat my way out.

It took, like, three hours to get it all out of my hair.

We finished making and baking our pizzas. Dad's pizza had sausage and green peppers. Mom made hers with sun-dried tomatoes and mushrooms. Mine had pepperoni.

I made sure there was an even number of pepperoni slices (thirty-two) on the whole pizza. There was also an even number of slices (eight). And an even number of pepperoni slices (four) on each piece.

"The Great Pizza Dough Catastrophe is one of my all-time favorite family memories," Dad said as he finished eating his final piece of pizza.

"Mine too," Mom said.

"And it all happened right here," I reminded them. "In *this* kitchen."

Everything was working out just right.

And I think they were thinking about all the nice things and memories.

There was only one clue to go.

And the timing was perfect.

I got the fourth clue out from where I'd hidden it—the microwave oven.

And right when I handed it to Dad, the doorbell rang. I knew who it was.

It was Rosie and Simon.

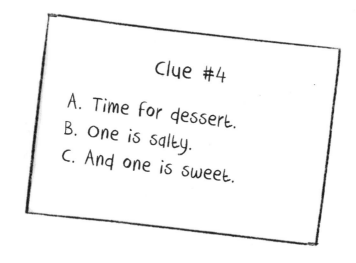

Clue #4

A. Time for dessert.
B. One is salty.
C. And one is sweet.

# CHAPTER TWELVE

# A LUMP IN MY THROAT

"HOW'S IT GOING?" Rosie said and handed me a takeout bag from Jethro's.

"Really good," I answered.

"Do you think you won't move now?" Simon asked and handed me a small paper bag. I knew there were chocolates inside.

"I don't know," I said honestly. "Mom and Dad are remembering a bunch of nice stuff.

Hummingbirds and bike rides and pizza-making. And, thanks to you guys, they're eating some of their favorite things from town."

"Molly!" Dad yelled from the kitchen. "Who's at the door?"

"You better go!" Rosie said.

And Simon said, "Good luck!"

I brought the french fries and chocolates back to the kitchen.

"It was Simon and Rosie again," I said, holding the bags behind my back. "They really helped me a lot."

"They're good friends," Mom said.

I just nodded because I got a lump in my throat when Mom said that. I thought about moving away from Rosie and Simon. And my eyes got watery too.

"I smell something familiar," Dad said and sniffed at the air in an exaggerated way. "French fries? From Jethro's?"

"Right," I said and brought his bag of fries out. I decided just to give Mom her chocolates from Barbo Brothers, because that lump was still there. I couldn't make it go away. I didn't want to talk. I couldn't dry up my eyes either.

And Mom and Dad noticed.

"Molly?" Mom asked and came closer. "Is something wrong?"

I shook my head.

"There *is* something wrong," Dad said. He came closer too.

I had to tell them. I couldn't keep it in any longer.

"I know what's going on."

"You do?" Mom asked.

"I heard you both Thursday morning," I said and sniffled. "I forgot my book report and had to run home to get it. I heard you talking upstairs while Mom was drying her hair."

"You already know?" asked Dad.

I nodded again. It was super hard to talk with that lump stuck in my throat.

"Well," Mom said. She was smiling a little bit—and I couldn't understand why. "What do you think about it?"

"I like our house," I whispered past that lump. "I'll miss Rosie and Simon *so* much. I don't want to move."

ONLY ONE MORE CHAPTER AND 513 WORDS LEFT TO GO! WHAT DO YOU THINK WILL HAPPEN?

# CHAPTER THIRTEEN

## THE LUMP DISAPPEARS

**"WAIT A MINUTE,** Molly," Dad said. His eyebrows were scrunched up a little. "What did you hear exactly?"

"That we're moving," I said and sat down at the kitchen table. My legs were wobbly.

"Molly," Mom said and sat down next to me on the right. "We're not moving."

"But I heard you say that you have to move all my stuff," I explained. That lump got a little smaller. "And move your stuff."

"We're not moving," Dad repeated.

"Not to a different place?" I asked and wiped my sleeve across my eyes. "Like to a new city or state or something?"

"We are going to move things around, just like you heard," Mom said. "But here in *this* house, not in a different house somewhere else."

I felt better, but I still didn't understand. "Why?"

"Well, we're going to change the rooms around upstairs," Dad explained. He was crouched down next to me on the left. "Right now, we have our room, your room, and the office that Mom and I use on the weekends for work sometimes. But we're going to change that."

"How?"

"We're going to move the office stuff downstairs. That room will become your room," Mom said. "It's a little bigger and has two windows instead of one. You can decorate it however you want."

"But I heard Dad say, 'We have to move,'"
I said. "That's a direct quote."

"I did?"

"Yes. I heard it. For sure."

They were quiet for a few seconds, trying
to remember their conversation.

"I know what you're talking about,
Molly," Mom said and giggled. "While I

was blow-drying my hair, Dad started to brush his teeth. And he reached in front of me and I walked behind him and the hair dryer cord got all tangled up between us. He said 'We have to move' because of that."

"It was all just a misunderstanding, Molly," Dad said.

"Really?!" That lump in my throat was totally gone. I was getting really happy now, but I still wasn't totally understanding. "But then why are we moving the rooms around and stuff? And what's happening to my room?"

Mom looked at Dad. And Dad looked at Mom. Then they both looked at me.

"It's becoming a nursery," Mom said and smiled.

I thought I knew that word, but I wasn't totally sure.

"It's going to be the new baby's room," Dad said.

That's what I thought that word meant!

"You're going to be a big sister," Mom said. She looked at me weird—like she wanted to know how I would react.

Dad looked at me the same way. He asked, "What do you think about that?"

"It's great!" I exclaimed. "I don't have to move away from Rosie and Simon! And it's great for another reason too."

"And what's that?" Mom asked. She stood next to Dad, who put an arm around her shoulder.

86

"We used to be a family of three!" I yelled. "But now we'll be a family of four! That's an even number!"

# HIGH FIVE!

You've read **13** chapters,

**87** pages,

and **5,995** words!

# Fun and Games!

## THINK

Draw your own food plate with sections. Do you have any creative sections like Simon? Do you have certain foods that you will definitely not eat like Molly?

## FEEL

Lots of families need to move. It happens all the time. Make a list of the three things you would miss the most about your home and neighborhood. Make a list of the three people you would miss the most. How would you stay in touch with them? Mail them weekly letters? Texting? Something else?

## ACT

Make your own game for your family. What clues would you use? What prizes would you give out?

Photo by Bill Kirby

**Tom Watson** is the author of the popular STICK DOG and STICK CAT series. And now he's the author of this new series, TROUBLE AT TABLE 5. Tom lives in Chicago with his wife and kids and their big dog, Shadow. When he's not at home, Tom's usually out visiting classrooms all over the country. He's met a lot of students who remind him of Molly, Simon, and Rosie. He's learned that kids are smarter than adults. Like, way smarter.

Photo by Krzysztof Wyżyński

**Marta Kissi** is originally from Warsaw but now lives in London where she loves bringing stories to life. She shares her art studio with her husband, James, and their pet plant, Trevor.